Mira Starling and the Mermaid Diaries

Prequel Story: The Tides of an Enchanted Tail

Abbix Publishing Company

© Copyright 2023 by Abbix Publishing Company - All rights reserved.

The content contained within this book may not be reproduced, duplicated, or transmitted without direct written permission from the author or the publisher.

Under no circumstances will any blame or legal responsibility be held against the publisher, or author, for any damages, reparation, or monetary loss due to the information contained within this book, either directly or indirectly.

Legal Notice:

This book is copyright protected. It is only for personal use. You cannot amend, distribute, sell, use, quote or paraphrase any part, or the content within this book, without the consent of the author or publisher.

Disclaimer Notice:

Please note the information contained within this document is for educational and entertainment purposes only. All effort has been executed to present accurate, up-to-date, reliable, complete information. No warranties of any kind are declared or implied. Readers acknowledge that the author is not engaging in the rendering of legal, financial, medical, or professional advice. The content within this book has been derived from various sources. Please consult a licensed professional before attempting any techniques outlined in this book.

By reading this document, the reader agrees that under no circumstances is the author responsible for any losses, direct or indirect, that are incurred as a result of the use of information contained within this document, including, but not limited to, errors, omissions, or inaccuracies.

Contents

1. First Day — 1
2. What Is Happening? — 6
3. The Unfolding — 16
4. Full Potential — 25
5. What Goes Around... — 32

Thank You Page — 36

Also By — 37

First Day

♥

Mira Starling, now sixteen years old, was determined to make her junior year of high school the best yet. The dark brown, long and wavy hair made her stand out in the crowd, and her piercing light brown eyes were warm but intimidating. She had a set plan for her school year, but she had no idea that her entire life was about to change.

Mira had a fun and bubbly personality, which made everyone around her admire and love her. Well, except the three most popular girls at her school, Emma, Nova, and Samantha. The hatred between the trio of girls and Mira had started way back when they were kids. Mira had always been the star student because of her high grades and the love her teachers had for her. Emma had always come second to Mira, and on the few occasions Emma had pulled ahead, she always tried to rub it in Mira's face, but she never got a reaction out of her.

Mira was happy for Emma's successes and even congratulated her every time she did better than her, so Emma's attempts never bothered her. This fueled Emma's hatred towards Mira and her friends, and she made sure that Nova and Samantha shared the same level of hatred towards them.

2

Today was the start of junior year, and Mira couldn't be more excited. She had a ritual with her mom since her first day of kindergarten, which was to always have breakfast together at the local bakery down the street from their house. She got up and got ready, putting minimal makeup on her face and wearing the sun dress she had picked out the day before.

"Mom, I'm ready! Let's go," Mira called for her mom as she ran down the stairs, impatiently wanting to start her day. She slipped on her sneakers and waited by the door.

Her mom came down the stairs, smiling warmly at her. The resemblance between her and her mom was uncanny due to their distinct facial features and their light hair.

"I'm here, honey," her mom said as she picked up her car keys and opened the door for both of them to go. "Mike told me that they started making salmon bagels for breakfast. It's so good that it's this month's bestseller. I'll give it a try. What are you going to order?"

They both got in the car, and Mira tapped her fingers nervously against her thighs. "You know that I hate seafood. I'll probably just order my regular grilled cheese sandwich and maybe a croissant," Mira explained to her mom as she played their favorite song on the car's speakers.

They had breakfast together, and chatted with Mike, the owner of the bakery and a family friend, for a little bit, and then her mom dropped her off at school where a familiar face approached.

"I missed you!" Mira shouted at her friend, Ava, as she hugged her tightly. Ava was Mira's first friend ever. They'd met on the first day of first grade, and they had been best friends ever since.

"You liar! We were just together two days ago," Ava giggled as she let go of Mira. Then, she sighed and rolled her eyes. "But I missed you too." Ava was never very emotional or really showed her feelings, but she always showed Mira her love through her loyalty and actions. Mira on the other hand was very expressive of her emotions and always loved to tell her friends and show them how much she loved and cared for them.

"So? I've missed you anyway," Mira jokingly teased her friend. "Have you seen Chloe or Fatima? I haven't seen Chloe since she came back from Europe. I missed her stupid questions," Mira asked Ava as they sat down on their bench where they'd sat since they were freshmen.

"I haven't seen her, but she texted me that she's coming today and to meet her at the four's bench," Ava stated. Their whole class called it the four's bench. It even had a number four engraved on the back.

The four were Mira, Ava, Fatima, and Chloe. Their class had started calling them that because they were always seen together, and the nickname had stuck.

"Hi, my loves, I missed you," Fatima excitedly announced, hugging both of her friends from behind the bench. "Oh my God! I haven't seen either of you for a week. My life was horrible."

Fatima dramatically fell down on the bench. She always loved adding a little bit of spice to everything. She was the drama queen of the four, but she argued that it was because of her love for acting and theater.

"Oh, Fatima, how we've missed how dramatic you are throughout this week." Ava threw her arm around Fatima. "Hope this doesn't make you fake cry or anything," she teased Fatima.

"Leave her alone. How's our favorite Lady Shakespeare doing?" Mira joked with her friend. Even though Ava was the closest to Mira, Fatima was Mira's secret keeper. Although she trusted all of her friends, she always confided in Fatima first and shared all of her secrets with her.

"Ha-ha, very funny. Where's Chloe? She said she'll be early. She wanted to tell us about Europe," Fatima wondered out loud.

"I'm right here," Chloe announced and giggled as all of her friends stood up and tightly hugged her. "I missed you, girls. Oh my God! There's so much to share with you and so little time to do so."

She sat down opposite her friends to start breaking down her entire trip for them. Chloe was the adventurous, hopeless romantic one. She romanticized every aspect of her life, fell in love with a new guy every week, and she always had a new story to share with the group, even though she saw them daily.

After a good fifteen minutes of Chloe debriefing her trip to her friends, they decided it was time to go to their lockers and walk to their classes. Just as they entered the door to the hallway and started walking to their lockers, they found Emma and Nova up in their faces.

"Oh, just what we needed for the day!" Ava sarcastically stated, rolling her eyes.

"My favorite four, hope you had a terrible summer," Nova said, giggling with her friend Emma.

Nova, unlike Samantha, had a backbone and a personality. She didn't just follow Emma around which intimidated Emma. However, she was heavily influenced by Emma's hatred for Mira. Nova had once been friends with Mira, but that had changed over the years when Nova and Emma became best friends.

"Nova, be nice," Emma sarcastically told Nova as they started walking away. Emma purposely bumped into Mira and spilled her strawberry juice all over Mira's dress.

"Oops." Emma and Nova started laughing and then walked away.

"My dress... What..." Mira stood there puzzled, wondering what she could do about her dress. "Why are they like that? I don't get it"

"She has always been like that." Ava tried to comfort a very shocked and upset Mira, "And don't worry, we'll find you something else to wear."

"I'm going to try out for the cheerleading team this year, and I am going to get in. I promise you that this year is our year," Mira said.

Her friends wanted to tell her that she'd probably never make the team because Emma was the captain, but none of them had the heart to crush her dreams.

"Come with me. I have a jacket in my bag. It will cover the stain. We'll just go clean you up, and then you can wear it," Fatima told Mira, grabbing her hand and walking with her towards the bathroom. "We'll meet you after first period, okay?"

Both Ava and Chloe nodded and headed to their lockers to put their books away.

When Mira and Fatima entered the bathroom, there stood Samantha.

"Are you a baby? Why do you have that all over you?" Samantha asked, holding in her laugh. Samantha was basically Emma's pet. If Emma told her to bark, she wouldn't hesitate.

"Your friend happened, and I swear, Sam, if you don't start running out of here..." Fatima scowled, and before she even finished her threat, Samantha ran out of the bathroom. "I feel bad for this girl, I swear."

"Put it out of your mind. Don't waste your time on them." Mira started wetting paper towels and trying to clean her dress. "She doesn't know any better than Emma's ways. I don't think she even knows why Emma's behavior is wrong."

"Your kindness is not always deserved, you know?" Fatima said and handed Mira her jacket.

What Is Happening?

♥

After a long day of classes, Mira finally got home. She texted her parents who were still stuck at work that she was home and she was going to be ordering pizza. The nature of her parents' work forced them to work long hours, and they got stuck working late most of the time. Her dad was a doctor, and her mom was the managing partner of a famous law firm. However, they were all very close, and it didn't keep them from spending time with her.

Mira had always felt like her parents' success was forcing her to be perfect, even though they never pressured her into putting in more work at school or tried to make plans for her future. In Mira's mind, it was because she had always been a grade A student, acing all of her classes, and participating in extracurricular activities. She always took on summer jobs since she turned twelve, starting with walking the neighbors' dogs, to working at their local movie theater.

Mira ordered a pizza and texted her friends to make sure they were all home safe. She then browsed through the internet, researching cheerleading dance routines and moves.

As she practiced in the living room, she had one thought in mind, *This year is my year.*

Her practice was cut short when the delivery guy rang the doorbell.

She opened the door, all sweaty from her routine, and she was met with Zayn, Emma's boyfriend.

"What happened to you?" he asked, chuckling as he handed her the pizza.

She stared at him, puzzled, wondering why Zayn was at her door, delivering her pizza.

"I'm trying to save up for a new phone because I broke mine, and my dad is too pissed to buy me a new one," Zayn answered as if he could read her thoughts. "So, you are running laps in there? You're soaked in sweat."

"I was practicing for the cheerleading tryouts. It's stupid, I know, and I might not get in. I probably won't, but I really want to give it a shot," Mira nervously explained, feeling embarrassed.

They had been very close friends when they were younger, but they had drifted apart when Zayn moved away for a while. Then, when he came back and started dating Emma a year ago, they stopped talking completely.

"I believe in you," he assured her as she gave him the money. "I miss you, Mira. I know you might think otherwise, but I'm always here for you."

"You wouldn't be dating Emma if that was true. Have a good night, Zayn," Mira said sharply and then slammed the door shut.

Zayn knew how poorly Emma treated Mira. Besides never doing anything to stop that, when Emma had told him that they could only date if he cut Mira off, he had done it. And Mira had sworn to never forgive him for that.

Despite all of the lonely days that Mira had lived after Zayn completely cut her off, she still had a soft spot for him, and that bothered her. Every time she saw him or had a bad day and wanted to talk to him, it made her feel frustrated and angry. Mira was a very bubbly person, and she did not like crying, causing scenes, or cutting someone off. The fact that Zayn was forcing her to feel those things made her even madder at him.

After Mira paid Zayn and closed the door, she went to wash her hands and face in the bathroom in her room. When she was washing her hands, just before she washed her face, she noticed that her hands were glowing under the water. It looked just like there was glitter dust on them, but she was sure she had no glitter on her. She pulled her hands out from under the faucet and dried them. They looked normal. She didn't think a lot about it, and she started washing her hands and face, but this time, her hands were glowing, and when she looked in the mirror, her face glowed as well.

"What the heck is going on...?"

She let it go, thinking to herself that she was probably just hungry enough to start seeing things. She exited the bathroom and put on a movie and started eating her pizza while waiting for her parents to come home.

"Mira, I'm home!" her dad called from the kitchen.

When she heard his voice, she ran out of her room and to the kitchen. Her dad had been stuck in the hospital for almost two days, and this was the first time he'd ever missed her first day of school.

As soon as Mira saw her dad in the kitchen, she ran and hugged him. "I missed you, Dad."

Mira was very close to both of her parents, and they were the type of family that sat together for dinner or breakfast every day. Not seeing her dad for two days was sort of a big deal for Mira.

As soon as she broke the hug with her dad, he noticed the droplets of water on her face and neck and how they were making her skin glow. His smile froze, and his eyes darted over her head as though he were looking for help.

"Is your mom home yet? I miss her," Mira's dad asked her as he sat down at the kitchen table.

'No, but she's supposed to be here in like fifteen minutes. She said she got Chinese food on her way back." Mira told her dad, reading the text that her mom had sent. She started noticing the worried expression on her dad's face. "Dad, is everything okay?" Mira asked.

"Yes, baby. I'm just a little bit hungry. I didn't eat after I got out of surgery. How was your first day of school?" Her dad asked.

"It was fine, just the usual. I'm planning on trying out for the cheerleading team. That's something new," she told her dad, sitting across from him.

"That's very nice, honey, but are you sure you can do that with all the extracurricular activities you are already doing?" Her dad frowned at her.

Mira's mom entered, interrupting their conversation. "Hi, I'm so sorry for taking so long. I got you food, too, honey." Mira's mom placed the food on the kitchen table. She kissed Mira on the cheek and asked about her day before hugging her husband.

Mira started telling them about her day in detail, before excusing herself to go finish her pizza that she'd left in her room.

When her dad was sure that she was in her room and could no longer hear them, he turned to look at his wife. "Her skin is starting to glow from water," he said with wide eyes.

"What? Are you sure?" Mira's mom asked, and her husband nodded. "Well, we need to prepare ourselves to have a talk with her very soon. If she doesn't know the truth, she might not be able to have control over herself," Mira's mom explained, and they both agreed that they were going to sit down with Mira the upcoming weekend and explain everything to her.

Midnight neared, and Mira was tossing and turning in her bed, trying to sleep, but her mind was racing, and her limbs were filled with trapped energy.

With a sigh of frustration, she rolled out of bed and went down to the kitchen to drink some water. After she chugged three glasses, she still felt thirsty.

"What's wrong with me?" Mira whispered to herself as she sat down on the kitchen counter and looked out their kitchen window. The small pool in their backyard glowed in the darkness, looking serene and inviting, and she decided that she would tire herself out with a good swim.

She ran upstairs, put on her bathing suit, and raced back to jump into the pool. The water surrounded her with its calm touch, and she started to swim from one end of the pool to the other. She had been swimming for a while when she looked up and saw that her mother was standing beside the pool, looking down at her daughter.

Her mom frowned at her, but she didn't seem surprised to see Mira swimming at such a strange hour. "Mira, it is one o'clock in the morning. What are you doing?"

"I couldn't sleep, and I felt like the pool was calling me," Mira giggled. "Come on, Mom. Join me, please," she whined and started splashing her mom with water.

"Mira, stop. Get out, now. Go take a shower, and go to sleep," her mom ordered, and Mira sighed before getting out of the water.

Mira's mom tried not to react, but her daughter's gorgeous glowing skin was very noticeable and she was worried Mira might see. She grabbed the towel and started quickly rubbing it against Mira's body to make sure she was dry, and Mira slowly stopped glowing.

"Mom! What are you doing? I can dry myself off." Mira started laughing at her mom who was treating her like a baby.

Mira went straight to the bathroom to take a shower.

Once she was under the running water, she noticed there were spots of scattered light moving on the bathroom walls. She jumped in place, and her eyes widened when she looked at her body and saw that she was glowing all over. Panic rising, she quickly jumped out of the shower, dried herself, and wrapped the towel around her body to go call her mom for help.

As she was passing by the bathroom mirror, she glanced at it and saw that she was no longer glowing. What was happening to her? She told herself that maybe she'd fallen asleep in the shower, and she was imagining it all. She decided to just go to bed and hopefully everything would be okay tomorrow. If she woke her parents up in the middle of the night, especially after her mom had to force her out of the pool, they would worry about her.

The next morning, Mira woke up incredibly thirsty. She pushed the cover off her body, and she screamed at what she saw. Large areas of her legs were covered in fish scales.

Both of her parents immediately ran to her room to see what's wrong, and just as they entered the room and asked what's wrong, Mira looked at her legs, and they were normal.

"I—I thought I saw... I had a bad dream" Mira lied, not knowing how to explain what she had just woken up to. Maybe it had been just a dream. Or maybe she was sick.

Her parents gave each other a knowing look, and her dad left the room. Her mom sat beside her and hugged her, assuring her that she was okay.

A few minutes passed by, and her dad came back into the room with a green drink and held it out to Mira.

"Drink this. You look a little pale, honey. It will help you get better," her mom told her.

Mira took the drink from her dad and chugged it, desperate to ease her thirst, and finally, she no longer felt like her mouth was dry.

Before leaving, her parents told her to wash up and get ready for school. Mira remembered her glowing skin, went into the bathroom, and placed her hands under running water. Nothing happened. She splashed her face with water and looked in the mirror. Again, nothing happened. Mira finally let out a deep breath and started her morning routine.

When she was done getting ready, she went down to the kitchen to have breakfast with her parents before school. "That drink, Dad, wow. It made me feel so much better. What was in it?" Mira asked before taking a bite from her sandwich.

"It's a family recipe, honey."

Although her dad hadn't really given her an answer, she was too focused on her sandwich to notice.

At school, as Mira made her way to her locker, she crossed paths with Zayn and Emma.

"Oh, look, it's the petty little cheerleader wannabe. I heard you wanted to try out. I hope you know that you're never getting in," Emma said condescendingly with a pout..

Mira ignored Emma's barbs, not wanting to give her the satisfaction. She just gave Zayn a look and continued walking to her locker.

"Hey, girl," Ava exclaimed as she opened her locker beside Mira's. "What's up with the sad face?"

Mira told her about her encounter a few minutes ago with Emma, and she was hesitant to tell her about Zayn's words the day before.

"I feel like you're hiding something. Tell me," Ava demanded.

Mira told her about what happened with Zayn the day before. "I miss him, Ava. I miss sharing my life with him. I miss having my friend," Mira sighed and pouted. "This morning, even after what he said yesterday, he didn't defend me when Emma was picking on me. He doesn't care. It's all an act for him."

"Look, Mira. I don't think that he's acting. He does care. That doesn't mean he deserves your friendship. He's a terrible friend. He does care, but he's terrible," Ava told Mira.

Ava always tries to look out for Mira. She hates that Mira forgave everyone, even people who didn't deserve it. However, Mira had a forgiving and forgetting mindset, and she always told her friends that they were all young and allowed to make mistakes. To Ava, some mistakes, no matter the circumstances, were unforgivable.

"What are we talking about?" Fatima and Chloe joined them at the lockers, but then the bell rang, and everyone dismissed the conversation.

As they were walking to class, Fatima and Chloe cooed about how Mira looked incredibly pretty today and tried to figure out what had changed. "I can't pinpoint what's actually different about you."

"Exactly, you're just radiating beauty at this point," Chloe complimented. "A goddess of beauty and grace. Your highness." She jokingly bowed down to Mira as they walked into class.

Mira spent that entire day getting complimented on her looks from everyone, even people she barely talked to. As they walked out of their last class of the day, Mira asked Fatima, "Is it just me, or am I getting a ton of compliments today that it's getting creepy?"

"You have been getting an odd number of compliments, but you also look eye-catchingly pretty today. It's unusual," Fatima said, and Mira jokingly glared at her. "No offense. You are a pretty girl, but today, you are head-turning pretty. You're 'looking at the girl that just walked in' kind of pretty," Fatima explained.

As the days passed, Mira found herself spending more time in the water, whether it was taking long showers or going for extended swims in her pool. She felt a very strong connection to the water, as if it was calling out for her and giving her energy. The more time she spent in the water, the more she felt as one with the water. She couldn't really comprehend what was happening.

More and more people around Mira started noticing the changes in her appearance. Her skin had taken on a radiant glow, her hair seemed to shimmer with a natural luster, and her gaze was always warm and inviting. Friends, teachers, and even strangers when she was out around town couldn't help but stop to compliment her on her beauty.

As the comments became more and more frequent, Mira started to wonder whether this whole thing was somehow connected to the scales she had seen on her legs before, the glow she had been experiencing because of water, or the changes she had noticed in her personality.

One thing that Mira couldn't understand about her new-found self was her interest in seafood. Mira had always hated seafood, and even the smell made her uneasy. However, for the entire week, she had been craving sushi, and she wanted to try it badly. When she shared this with her friends, they were very surprised, but they agreed that they would take her out to eat sushi on Friday if she still wanted to.

Mira's dad was consistent with giving her the green drink that he had given her before, and she loved it. After all this time without any more strange things popping up on her body, Mira was starting to forget about the scales and the glow.

Friday came around, and as promised, her three friends took her to their favorite sushi restaurant. As they sat around in the cozy restaurant, Mira had no idea which sushi rolls to order, so her friends helped her out.

As soon as the food arrived at the table Mira dove in, and she was loving every single piece she was having. Her friends were shocked, but they were too happy about this development to question her.

"Finally, you got rid of your childish taste buds," Chloe congratulated Mira, and they all laughed.

The Unfolding

♥

Saturday morning, Mira's parents called her into the living room, their expressions of a mix of concern and anticipation. Mira could sense that something was wrong when she saw the worry on their faces. She took a seat across from where her parents were sitting on the coach.

"Mira, we need to have a serious conversation," her dad began, his voice filled with love and determination. "There are things about our family's history that we have kept hidden from you, but we believe it's time for you to know the truth."

Mira's heart raced, and she looked from her dad to her mom, her eyes filled with a mixture of excitement and apprehension. "What is it? What have you been hiding from me?" Mira asked. After a moment of silence, she joked, "Are we vampires?"

Her parents exchanged a glance. Taking a deep breath, her mom spoke gently yet firmly. "Mira, you are not entirely human. Our family has a deep connection to a world beyond our own—a world of mermaids."

Mira's smile dropped.

"Mermaids? You mean they're real?" Both of her parents nodded their heads. "Are you guys pranking me? This isn't funny."

Her dad nodded, his eyes filled with concern. "Yes, Mira. Mermaids are real, and you are part of that lineage. That's why you've been experiencing these changes and feeling a deep connection to water."

Mira stood up and started pacing around their living room. Her mind raced, trying to process what she was hearing. The mysterious compliments, her love for water, and the physical transformations—it was all beginning to make sense. "So, I'm a mermaid? How is that possible?"

"Well, we both are related to the underwater world, and since you have our blood, you're one too." Her mom tried to explain, "It's not a given that if two people with mermaid blood have a child, that child would be a mermaid, but it's very likely. But according to the underwater world rules, we're not allowed to share our history with our children until it's confirmed they are a mermaid."

Her dad reached out for her mom's hand. "We put the mermaid world at risk of being discovered by humans, that's why we hid it from you. The drink we have been giving you is used to disguise visible mermaid powers for twenty-four hours. We were worried about your powers developing before we could teach you. We are really sorry."

"I thought I was going crazy, that I was imagining things, and you're sorry?" Mira sat down again. "I want to know everything. Explain everything to me now! Am I going to turn into a fish? Do you guys have tails?" Mira started, firing questions at light speed.

"We do have fishtails. You do, too. However, we will need to teach you how to transform and how to control your transformation. If you don't know how to control yourself, any splash of water might turn you into a mermaid and that's dangerous," her dad explained.

"Mira, you're not allowed to talk to anyone about this or share it with any of your friends. It's against the rules to tell anyone about our secret. There will be consequences if anyone ever found out about us," Mira's mom warned her.

"Oh, don't worry. Even if I wanted to share this with anyone, they'd call me crazy right away." Mira laughed and started to calm down a little bit. "Do we know any other mermaids? Or mermen?" Mira questioned.

Her parents gave each other a look and told her that there was no one else that she knew.

Mira knew right away that her parents were lying, but she decided to let it go. At least for the duration of this conversation. Later, she could investigate this on her own.

Her parents promised to answer any questions she might have moving forward, but asked her to give them time to teach her how to control her transformation. They said that they would help her understand the importance of her powers and when and why she should use them. The only point they had stressed was that she could never use her powers, or skill enhancements around humans.

The entire time her parents were talking to her, she had just one thought: when will she be able to share this huge secret with her friends. Were they even going to believe her? Her head hurt trying to imagine the consequences her friends might face, and that was the only thing keeping her from bolting out of her seat and calling Fatima to share everything with her.

After a long and tiring conversation, Mira excused herself and went to her room. Right as she closed her bedroom door, she grabbed her laptop and tried to find everything she could about the mermaid world.

At first, all she could find was fairytale nonsense and cosplay photo shoots, but after an hour of scouring the internet, she came upon an old book. She tried to access the link, but it had a validation process that stopped her from her search. Perhaps her parents' bookcase contained any mermaid related books or knowledge, and if that failed she was going to go to the local library near her house to find that mysterious book.

She took a picture of the book cover with her phone and memorized the title to see if she could find it at any of the places that sold books. She tried one last time to find it online, but the only version she could find was the one requiring validation.

Mira was so engrossed in her task that she didn't hear her mom knock on the door or enter her room. "Honey, your dad and I are going out. Do you need anything?" she asked. Mira's eyes widened momentarily before she assumed a nonchalant look on her face. Now that her parents were out of the way, she decided that she was going to search the entire house for any information that she could get on the mermaid world.

"No, mom. Thank you. Just get me food on your way home," Mira requested, and smiled warmly at her mom. Her mom nodded and closed the bedroom door behind her. Mira waited till she heard the front door slam shut, then she jumped out of her bed.

She raced to her parent's home office, and pushed the door open. Going right to the book case, Mira started searching for the book that she had seen online, or any book that was related to mermaids, or marine life in general. Yet she found nothing.

She wanted to search each book more closely, but was scared that her parents would know that she went through their stuff. She searched every drawer in that room, but also came up empty handed.

The next logical place for her to look was her parents' bedroom. She tried to look there as much as she could without making a mess, but, again, her search was fruitless.

What Mira didn't know was that her parents hadn't coincidentally left her alone. They knew that Mira would search the entire house for any mermaid related things, given the chance, so they hid everything in a place that Mira had no idea of accessing. That way, Mira would find nothing that they didn't want her finding that might give her knowledge she wasn't prepared with dealing with yet.

After an hour of searching the entire house, Mira was very tired, and decided to call it a day. She was sure that there was stuff hidden inside the house, but she knew that her parents hid them well. She knew that if she kept searching, she would find nothing, as long as her parents didn't want her finding anything.

The next day, Mira woke up early, had breakfast and went to the local library near her house. She wanted to get out of the house before her parents woke up to make sure that she wouldn't need to explain where she was going that early on a Sunday morning.

She swiped her library ID, and entered the building. She was met with the front desk lady who smiled politely at her, and Mira returned the smile. She mouthed a "good morning" to the lady, and went ahead to the science fiction area of the library, beginning her search there.

She searched the shelves of each department for any book that didn't look like it was a novel, a children's book, or a fiction book. After 15 minutes of thoroughly searching through the shelves, she came upon a hardcover book that looked very old. It didn't have an author or a title. Not ones that she could understand, anyway. Etched onto the cover of the book were strange markings lined up next to each other. Those must be letters, I guess.

The letters on the cover of the book looked like runes or drawings. The edges of the hardcover, and the pages inside the book were deteriorated. The words inside the book were written in a language that she couldn't recognize, but the letters were normal Latin letters.

MIRA STARLING AND THE MERMAID DIARIES

Mira decided to take that book home and try to translate it there, and kept on searching for any other books that would aid in her search for answers. She had no luck finding any more books in the science fiction section, so she moved on to the history section.

Suddenly, her eyes spotted a book that looked familiar, so she unlocked her phone and looked for the picture she had taken of the book she had found online, and found them to be very similar but not identical. When she opened the book that she had found in the library, its pages were completely blank pages, although as she was flipping through them, they felt rough, like they had something engraved on them.

She traced down a page with her fingers, and felt the outline of letters. These books needed further investigation at home, so Mira went over to the register to take out both books. When she was done, she placed the books in her backpack and left to go home.

Once at home, Mira was surprised to find her mom waiting for her. "Where were you, Mira? Why didn't you tell me you were going out?" Her mom worriedly questioned her.

"I woke up early and decided to go for a walk, so I returned some books I had borrowed from the library on the way," Mira partially lied to her mother. She didn't want to lie about where she was because she knew both of her parents had access to her location through her phone, and she knew that her mom had probably checked it.

"I was worried, honey. Next time, let me know you'll be going out the night before. Or at least text me before leaving the house." She nodded at her mom, who came over to hug her and wish her a good morning.

Mira excused herself and went straight to her room. She could sense that her mom suspected her behavior, so she hid the books well and separately from one another. She wanted to make sure that even if her parents found one, she would still have the other one.

Throughout her morning shower, Mira was mesmerized by how her skin glowed under the water. She noticed the scales appearing all over before disappearing again, and she smiled. She loved and accepted every single thing that made her who she was.

After getting out of the shower, dressing in comfortable clothes, and putting her hair in a bun, Mira went down to sit with her parents. Before leaving her room, she checked on the books one more time to make sure they were where she had left them.

Relieved, Mira descended to join her parents, who were waiting for her with one question: Are you ready to learn more about her skills? Mira's face lit up with excitement, and she nodded and ran to sit down on the couch. "Well, first off, let me remind you that you can't use your powers around humans. No matter how subtle you might think you are, humans might start noticing a pattern and suspect something." Mira's dad explained the dangers of mermaids using their powers in public.

Mira nodded, showing that she understands the risks of using her powers in public. "There are two kinds of powers: enhancements and strengths. Enhancements are the things that humans can do as well, but to a limited degree basically, whatever they can do, you can do better. You can run faster, jump higher, hear better and react faster. You can obviously swim better as well, but this is basically a mix of both which we'll go over in detail later," Mira's mom explained.

"Strengths are things that you can do as mermaid that humans can't. You can breathe under water; you can have scales that help you navigate under water. You can enchant anyone with your voice, but that's a power that not all mermaids have, and needs much practice. You can transform to your mermaid body, but it doesn't work like it does in movies. You need to want to transform in order for it to happen, among other things. You can also shape and transform things in their liquid form, but that will need practice as well."

"Do mermaids speak a certain language? Other than English, I mean," Mira asked her parents trying to figure out the language she had seen on the book earlier.

"In ancient times, mermaids used to speak a mermaid language called Mermish, but now they speak normal English," Mira's dad explained. "The language of Mermish was a little bit too complicated to learn and understand. Of course, we'll teach you all about the Mermish language, but it's not a priority at the moment."

"Back to enhancements! You can use your enhancements starting now. Try to jump higher and you'll be able to do it. Try to run faster, and you'll be able to do it. Try anything that you were doing as a human, and you'll find out you can do it better, but you can't do any of that around humans, it will look abnormal, Mira," Mira's mom explained and then warned her.

"Okay, I get it, I promise. What about my strengths? How do I use them?" Mira asked, eager to know. "Will my skin always glow underwater? Will I always develop scales randomly?"

"You get scales when you're stressed or exposed to water. We will teach you how to control your skin's reaction to water and stress. Until we do, you can always use the green drink to control your skin's reaction," Mira's dad offered. "As for your strengths, we'll start teaching you everything next weekend. Some things won't take a long time, like transforming. Other things might take a longer time, or never happen, like enchanting"

"Okay. Now to put my skills to the test," Mira said standing up and ran to her room. She did run a lot faster than she normally did, and what's more that it wasn't tiring for her.

Now that she was alone, Mira locked her bedroom door and opened her laptop, searching for any translation tools from Mermish to English. After sifting through a lot of dead ends, Mira stumbled onto a website that hadn't been updated since 2012. It looked legit.

Grabbing the book with the invisible engravings, Mira began tracing each letter until she could make them out. She typed the things that were written on the cover page, and pressed enter. She read out loud the translation, "To all Crystalices, Waterglows, Neros, and Starlings". The moment she saw her name, she knew that she had found the answers she had been looking for. And they were all contained in this book.

She used the pencil to make the words more visible, so she could understand them, and started translating the pages, taking notes all over the book. After an hour of researching had passed, Mira realized that she hadn't found any additional information than what her parents had provided.

Mira started googling the last names that she found on the cover page of the book, and the first thing that came up was a Facebook page of someone called Zayn; Zayn Nero. However, Mira was so focused on her own last name that she failed to recognize Zayn's.

Did her parents know about Zayn? Does Zayn know about her? Does Zayn know that he's not entirely human? Those were all questions racing through her mind.

Full Potential

♥

After finding out about Zayn, Mira didn't know what to think. She didn't know who to confide in, or who to trust. She knew her parents would lie to her, or attempt to hide the full truth. All this worry caused her skin to break out in scales, so she decided to end her search for the truth for now, realizing just how fast the tiring day had caught up to her.

The next day at school, Mira went to put her name down for cheerleading tryouts, before placing her backpack in her locker. She saw Zayn talking to his friends and stared at him, wondering whether he knew that he was a merman, or if he even knew anything about the mermaid world.

Suddenly, Mira's thoughts were interrupted by Emma high-pitched voice. "Why are you staring at my boyfriend?" Emma pushed Mira against her locker and stared right into her eyes.

"I wasn't, Emma. I zoned out, I didn't know what I was looking at," Mira said standing up straight, balancing herself. "Stop thinking that the whole world revolves around you. We all have our own lives to worry about. No one is obsessed with you." Mira silently thanked God that she had drank the green juice before leaving for school, because she was sure that by now, she'd be covered in fish scales.

"Flash news: the world does revolve around me, and everyone is obsessed with me." Emma smirked as she spoke the words confidently. As Emma was about to turn around to join her boyfriends, she spoke again, "I saw your name on the tryouts list. I promise you, you'll never make the team, so don't bother showing up. Save yourself the embarrassment, love."

Mira ignored Emma, and just rolled her eyes. She knew that, with her newly acquired powers, she could definitely make the team. Everyone would think that she had simply been practicing, and not the fact that she had supernatural powers.

Once more someone brought her back to reality, but this time it was Ava hugging her. "You went MIA the entire weekend. Where have you been?" Ava asked, looking a little bit worried.

"Home. I decided to spend the weekend with my parents. I'm fine, I promise. I've also been practicing a lot for tryouts. I'm pretty much a pro by now," Mira proudly informed her friend.

"Go, Mira! I'm sure you'll get in. I'm even surer that it might give Emma a heart attack." Both girls giggled as they started walking to class together, where they met up Fatima and Chloe.

When Mira went home, her mom was standing in the kitchen, cooking dinner and waiting for her. "Hi, Mom." Mira placed her bag on the floor and sat down on the kitchen stool.

"Hi, baby. Dinner is almost ready. Your dad is stuck at work and won't be back till late tonight," Mira's mom informed her.

Right then and there, Mira got an idea. "Mom... after we eat dinner, do you mind teaching me a little bit about transforming?" Her mom paused for a second, then turned to face Mira.

"Why don't you just wait for the weekend, Mira? Your dad and I will teach you then. Somewhere more appropriate than our kitchen," her mom explained, then went back to cooking. So, Mira decided to let it go for now and change her clothes and wash up for dinner. She quickly locked her bedroom door and started looking through the book that she hadn't looked through yet. She opened her laptop and started translating random pages from the middle which happened to be talking about mermaid realms. At first, Mira thought that mermaid realms were just areas of the ocean where mermaids would swim or stay, but upon reading further, she came to understand that all mermaid houses were built over water realms that gave them access to the ocean.

Mermaid realms were hidden under houses but were easily accessed by all mermaids that knew how to find and access them. The goal of mermaid realms was to give mermaids access to the ocean, and a place where mermaids could hide their oceanic belongings from the humans.

Mira slammed her laptop shut and went to look for her mom, finding her in the living room, and angrily spoke through her teeth. "Where's our realm?" her mom's face turned white like she just saw a ghost.

"What are you talking about, Mira? There is no such thing as 'realms'!" Her mom got nervous and stood up.

"Mom, stop lying to me! Why are you hiding this from me?" Mira shouted past the tears that were running down her face. After a long screaming match, Mira's mom finally gave in and took her down to the basement.

Her mom pressed on a button on the wall, then pushed a small panel to the side. When the door/wall was out of the way, Mira saw a stony hallway that seemed to go on forever. Mira followed her mom down a few steps that lead into the hallway, until they got to a room made of stone.

The room was full of sea objects, and smelt like the ocean. There were a few sitting areas, and at the corner of the big realm she could see a small pool, where the ocean smell was strongest.

"Here you go," her mom spoke calmly. "This is our realm. We come her to swim, or to gain safe access to the ocean. Do you want me to teach you how to fully transform to mermaid form?" she asked.

After a couple hours of instructions and trials, Mira and her mom both transformed to full mermaid form and swam around their small pool. Out of the blue, Mira saw her dad swim in through their ocean access, and he was shocked when he saw Mira. "You got your tail?" her dad said in awe.

"I got my tail," Mira confirmed. She splashed the water with her tail and giggled. Mira's parents took her for a swim in the ocean, and they never felt closer as a family than they did at that moment.

After a long time of learning how to control her skin and her transformations, and how to control liquids, Mira finally went to sleep in her bedroom, feeling more satisfied than she ever had. Before drifting off, thoughts of Zayn came to mind, and whether he truly was part.

The next day was tryouts day, and Mira couldn't be more excited. As she began her warm-up stretches in the gym, Samantha came in and informed them of what was expected of them during tryouts. By the end of the day, they would be announcing the girls that made it onto the team. She also let them know of the final phase the next day, where the teachers would make the final decision of whether the eligible girls that the team had picked out from tryouts actually fit the criteria.

The first routine was just a simple routine, to show whether the girls had the flexibility and seamlessness they needed. Mira passed easily without having to use her powers at all. The second routine was to show how many flips they could do in a row, and whether they could do them correctly. Again, Mira passed without having to use her mermaid powers.

The final routine was the hardest, but Mira was confident. Despite her confidence, Mira wanted to make sure that she would pass that routine, so she relied on her powers to get her through flawlessly; which they did. Samantha and Nova were impressed, whereas Emma was fuming at Mira's perfect routine.

"You think you're so perfect? How about this. If you do this routine correctly, you are on the team, but if you fail, you can never try out for the team again." To Mira, the logical thing was to refuse that offer, yet armed with her new-found confidence, she found herself accepting.

Her friends kept telling her that it was a stupid move, but she didn't listen and followed up. "I only have one condition. You can't be the one to judge my performance." Emma accepted Mira's condition, assured that Mira wouldn't be able to perform her hard routine.

Emma started the routine and when she was done, everyone in the gym was talking about how hard the routine was. Mira's friends started to worry that Mira might not be able to perform it correctly, and they started to panic.

Mira did the routine correctly, and maybe even better than what Emma did. Everyone was surprised, and Emma looked at Samantha and Nova waiting for them to tell Mira that she failed, "Girl, you're definitely a part of the team. How did you pull this off so effortlessly?" Samantha asked, causing Emma to glare at her.

"Are you kidding me? That was horrible. She definitely failed!" Emma said, but no one was listening.

After a long and tiring day, Mira finally went home. "How did the tryouts go?" Mira's mom asked and Mira told her everything, only leaving out the parts about her using her power.

Her mom was very proud of her, and told her how proud her dad would be. Mira made her way to their underground realm, and after transforming, swam out into the ocean. She knew that her friends were hanging out at Ava's house by the ocean, and decided to swim there to join them.

When she arrived, however, she was shocked to find her friends swimming in the ocean, and they had almost spotted her. Immediately, Mira swam back to the safety of her realm and didn't look back. When her friends investigated were Mira had been, they couldn't find anything and they didn't think longer about it.

When Mira arrived at the pool in the realm, her human form returned the moment she stepped out of the water. She ran out of the realm and pressed the button to hide the doorway, terrified to tell her parents what had happened. Finally, she decided not to tell them.

Mira entered her bedroom, her mom coming in right after. "Honey, the Nero's will be joining us for dinner. Your dad just told me, so start getting ready. They're almost here," she informed Mira, who just nodded.

This would be the perfect opportunity to find out whether Zayn knew about the mermaid world or not. She got ready, and as she descended the stairs, the doorbell rang. Her dad opened the door for their guests, and her mom came out of the kitchen to greet them.

The Starling's told the Nero's to wash up and join them at the dining table. After the families had dinner and dessert was served, Zayn and Mira went out to sit down by the pool and talk. "I heard you finally got your tail," the second the words left his mouth, Mira was speechless. All the questions running through Mira's mind were answered, as soon as Zayn had spoken.

"You... how?" Mira was shocked, and she felt a little bit betrayed. She understood why her parents might have hidden all that from her, but why had Zayn?

"That's why I drifted away from you, Mira. It wasn't for Emma. After I found out, I couldn't keep lying to your face, and your parents asked me to not tell you till you started showing signs of transformation," Zayn explained, and everything suddenly clicked in her mind.

"You never betrayed me," she spoke softly. Zayn sat down beside her and hugged her. "I missed you."

"I'm sorry, Mira. I'm sorry I wasn't there. I'm sorry," Zayn sobbed into Mira's hair. They both spent the entire night catching up and talking about the boring and not-so boring details of their lives.

Emma always knew that Zayn would eventually return to be friends with Mira again, and it always made her jealous of Mira. That morning she caught Zayn watching Mira during tryouts, which did nothing but fuel her deep-seated jealousy for Mira.

What Goes Around...

♥

The next morning, Mira woke up early to get ready for the day. There was another phase of cheerleading tryouts. The importance of that phase was to show the teachers your skills, and they would get to decide what your role would be on the team, or they would deem you unfit.

Mira was as ready as she could ever be. She arrived at school, and went right to her friends at the gym. "Good morning," Mira told her friends, and they all smiled at her. "You will never believe what I'm about to say."

They all gave her a puzzled look, and before any of them could ask what she meant, Zayn spoke from behind her. "Good morning, Mira. Good morning, girls."

They all mouthed a good morning, and before anyone could say anything else, Mira's teacher called for the new members of the team. Unfortunately, Emma had seen what had happened, and her blood boiled at the sight of Zayn talking to Mira. Yet before she could confront him, the teacher asked her to join them inside.

All the new members were asked to do a routine of their choice, including a routine that Emma performed for them. The second routine was performed in groups, with current team members serving as back-up for the try outs.

When it was Mira's turn to perform, she did the routine of her choice flawlessly. The teachers were impressed and applauded her. Mira was assigned Samantha, Nova and Emma to back her with her routine. This was Emma's chance.

As they were performing, Emma let Mira fall, but made it seem like Mira messed up. When their teacher was about to disqualify Mira, Nova spoke up, "it was Emma's fault. Emma let her fall on purpose, I swear."

"Is that true?" their teacher asked, looking at Emma. Emma kept denying everything, until Samantha spoke up to support Nova's story.

"Oh, Emma! I'm beyond shocked. You're benched for a week. No trainings, no performances and no nothing!" their teacher angrily informed Emma.

"But I'm the team captain! You can't bench me!" Emma tried to argue back.

"Samantha will only be replacing you for the week. Don't worry about the team," her teacher sarcastically said.

Mira was allowed a second chance to perform the routine, after the teacher assigned her someone other than Emma, and this time, she performed it perfectly.

Because of how good Mira was, she was the first girl to be accepted onto the team. She ran over to celebrate with her three friends, and Zayn went over to congratulate her. As she was talking to Zayn, Samantha and Nova also joined in with congratulations.

As Mira went to the locker room to get changed, she didn't notice Emma follow her inside. "You!" Emma shouted. "You want to steal my boyfriend, my friends and my team!"

"Emma, calm down! No one wants to steal anyone from you!" Mira explained stepping away from Emma, who looked like she was about to attack her.

"I saw you! You were flirting with Zayn. I know you are in love with my boyfriend, so just admit it!" Emma shouted, getting closer to Mira, who was terrified.

"Zayn is like a brother to me. We are just family friends. The team and your friends are all your own doing. You let me fall. You tried to sabotage me," Mira explained. Mira was starting to get angry, but she also knew that her emotions were wild and that she was much stronger and more powerful than Emma. She could end up hurting her.

"You always take away everything from me. Just live your own life and leave me alone," Emma said and tried to push Mira, but Mira didn't budge.

"For your own good, Emma, get away from me. Oh, and believe me, if I wanted to steal anything or anyone from you, I would have already," Mira confidently stated, before leaving Emma standing there.

With nothing else to say, Emma left the locker room and went to find Zayn and her friends. She found Nova and Samantha first and charged at them with fury. "You're, traitors! You betrayed me! You sided with Mira!" Emma shouted at them, and they both took a step back.

"We didn't side with anyone. She's an asset for the team, Emma, you just need to get over yourself and let this whole thing go," Samantha explained to Emma, calmly.

"You are my friends. Why do you care about her?" Emma asked, calming down and looking hurt.

"We don't care about her. We care about the team, and as of now, she's a part of the team. You need to be a team player, Emma." Nova finally found her voice. "If you keep up this behavior, the rest of the team might not pick you as head of the team for this semester, Emma. Treat the entire team equally, and show them that you can get over your differences with the members, for the best interest of the team."

Nova's words convinced Emma to be civil towards Mira. Well, not actually civility, but fake civility in front of the team. She promised herself to come up with a plan to sabotage Mira, without the plan ever being traced back to her.

A Heartfelt THANK YOU

Your decision to purchase and read our book fills us with immense happiness and gratitude. We embarked on this writing endeavor with a vision to inspire, entertain, and touch the lives of our readers. We hope that the world we've created within these pages of our book has captured your imagination and left a lasting impression.

We humbly ask that you take a moment to leave a review on the website where you purchased our book from. Your honest and heartfelt feedback is invaluable to us as authors.

 In addition, we invite you to join our community by signing up on our website. Once you've signed up, you will gain exclusive access to a free 50-question-and-answer trivia challenge. But that's not all. By becoming a member of our community, you will be among the first to receive notifications about new stories featuring **Mira Starling**.

Thank you for allowing us to be a part of your reading experience. We sincerely hope that our book has brought you joy, awe, and moments of inspiration.